A
Firefly
Named

TORCHY

A
Firefly
Named

TORCHY

by

Bernard Waber

1970 Houghton Mifflin Company Boston

J
PB

for

Bonni

Jill

and

Eric

A
Firefly
Named
TORCHY

O n a warm night,
at the edge of a woods,
a firefly was born.
His name was Torchy.

"Eat your dinner," his mother
would say, when Torchy was just
a little flicker, "and some day you
will grow up as big and as bright
as your father."

Torchy did eat his dinner,
and did grow up big and bright.
Everyone was astonished, his light
was so bright.

"Whatever did he eat?" the other mother
  fireflies wanted to know.
"Just the usual nectar, pollen, slugs —
  that sort of thing," Torchy's mother answered.
But she was as surprised as the next firefly.

Early, each night, the fireflies
came out to dance.
They loved to show off their lights, and
flash secret messages to one another.
They twinkled and glowed, and together made
a thousand chandeliers in the woodland.

Torchy, too, wanted to show off,
to twinkle and glow and flash
secret messages.

But when Torchy turned on his light . . .
suddenly, just as bright as day,
there was Mouse,
and there was Fox,
and there was Rabbit,
and there was Squirrel,
and there was Possum,
and there was Skunk,
and there was Beaver,
and there was Frog.

And Mouse looked at Fox,
and Fox looked at Rabbit,
and Rabbit looked at Squirrel,
and Squirrel looked at Possum,
and Possum looked at Skunk,
and Skunk looked at Beaver,
and Beaver looked at Frog.
And everyone was so surprised
to see everyone.

Click beetles fell on their
backs, they were so surprised.

Flowers, with petals folded
for the night, unfolded again.

Baby birds, thinking it morning,
cried out to be fed.

Earthworms, up for the evening,
scrambled for cover.

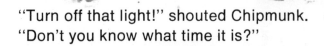

"Turn off that light!" shouted Chipmunk.
"Don't you know what time it is?"

"Turn off that light!" shouted Woodchuck.
"Now, I'll be tired in the morning."

"Turn off that light!" shouted the other
 fireflies, hiding deep in the grass.
"You are supposed to be softly twinkling,
 you know!"

"TURN OFF THAT LIGHT,"
 everyone shouted at once.

Torchy turned off his light.
It was dark again.
Everyone was happy . . .
everyone but Torchy.

"If only I weren't so bright.
If only I could softly twinkle,
like the other fireflies," Torchy sighed.
"Nonsense!" his mother answered, from her resting
place on top of a blade of grass. "Any one can twinkle.
All you must do is take your time about it. That's all.
And when you are ready to twinkle, breathe deeply and
think happy, twinkly thoughts."

"Like this!" said his mother, taking a deep breath.
 Magically, her golden light began at once to twinkle.
"That's beautiful!" Torchy exclaimed.
"See!" said his mother. "What did I tell you? Nothing
 to it. Right? Now, you go out and try it yourself."
"Oh, I will!" Torchy answered eagerly.
"And Torchy," said his mother, "just say to
 yourself, I can twinkle."
"I can twinkle," said Torchy.
"Say it again."
"I can twinkle!"
"Again."
"I CAN TWINKLE!"
"Good!" said his mother,
"and good luck!"

So Torchy went out again.
And he remembered to take his time.
And he remembered to breathe deeply.
And he remembered to think happy, twinkly thoughts.
And slowly, ever so slowly, he tried to twinkle.

But when he did . . .
suddenly, as bright as day,
there was Mouse,
and there was Fox,
and there was Rabbit,
and there was Squirrel,
and there was Possum,
and there was Skunk,
and there was Beaver,
and there was Frog.

And Mouse looked at Fox,
and Fox looked at Rabbit,
and Rabbit looked at Squirrel,
and Squirrel looked at Possum,
and Possum looked at Skunk,
and Skunk looked at Beaver,
and Beaver looked at Frog.
And everyone was surprised all
over again.

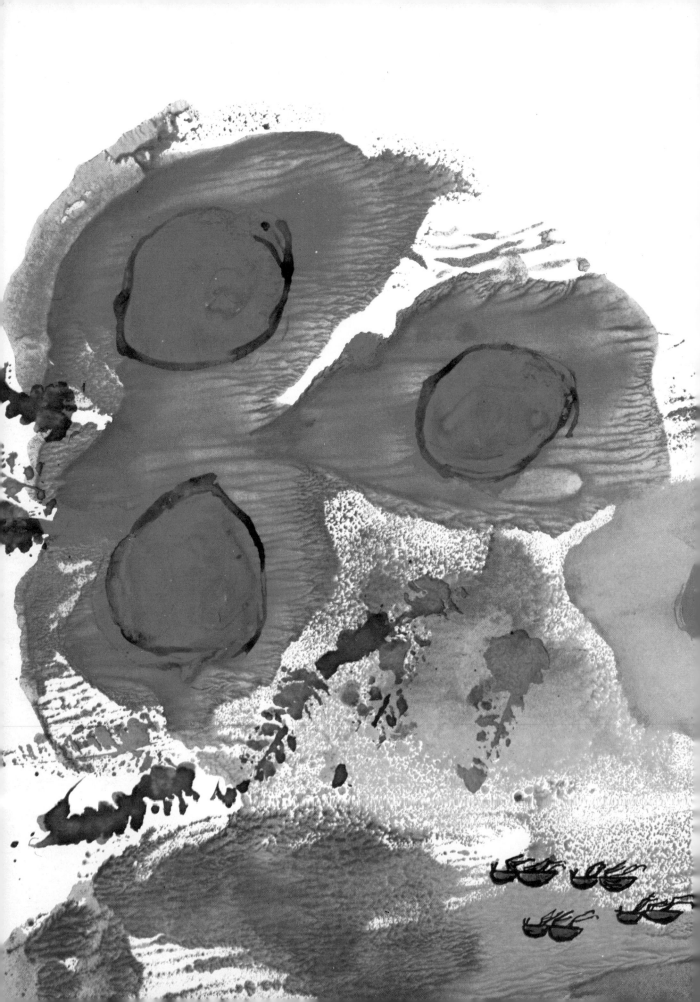

Flowers unfolded their petals,
all over again.

Click beetles fell on their backs,
all over again.

Baby birds cried to be fed,
all over again.

And the earthworms scrambled for cover,
all over again.

"Turn off that light!" shouted Chipmunk.
"Turn off that light!" shouted Woodchuck.

"Turn off that light!"
shouted the other fireflies.
"TURN OFF THAT LIGHT!"
everyone shouted at once.

Torchy turned off his light.
It was dark again.
Everyone was happy . . .
everyone but Torchy.

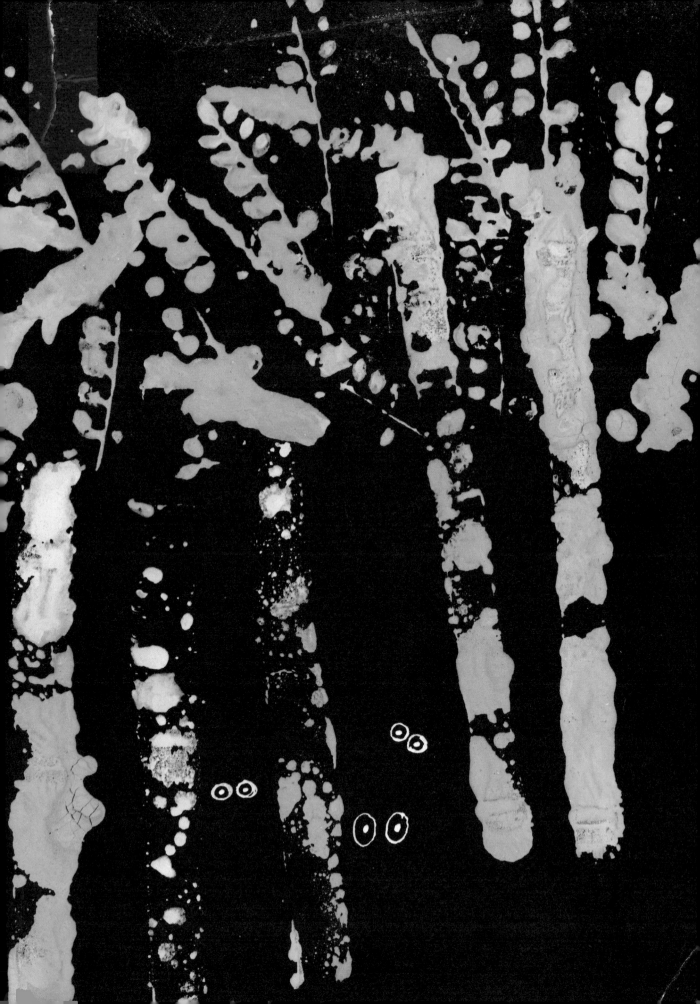

"If only I weren't so bright.
  If only I could softly twinkle," Torchy sighed.
"Nobody is perfect," Owl spoke up. "Perhaps,
  you weren't meant to twinkle."
"But I want to twinkle," said Torchy.
"Look at it this way," said Owl. "There are
  many kinds of light in the world. You should
  be mighty proud of yours, Torchy."
"But I want to twinkle," said Torchy.
"What is so special about twinkling? You can
  find twinklers anywhere."
"But I want to twinkle," said Torchy.
"Torchy, yours is like no other firefly light —
  in the whole, wide world. Do you know what that means?"
"It means I can't twinkle," said Torchy.
"And you want to twinkle," said Owl.
"Yes," Torchy answered.
"Think it over, Torchy," said Owl.

Torchy flew away to think.
"Why shouldn't I twinkle?" he thought. "I'm a
firefly, aren't I? Fireflies are supposed to twinkle.
That's what we're here for: to twinkle.
"Besides," he thought, "it's nice to twinkle. And it's
fun to twinkle. Happiness is twinkling," he decided,
"especially for fireflies."

Torchy was still carried away in thought, when
suddenly he was surprised by the many dancing lights
off in the distance. "There must be millions of fireflies
out there!" he exclaimed to himself.
Torchy decided to join them.

Soon, he was surrounded by lights . . .
all manner of lights . . .

big lights,
little lights,
bright lights,
dim lights,
yellow,
blue,
green,
orange,
red,
purple,
and
white lights . . .

dazzling, zooming, zipping, zigzagging lights . . .
and yes, even twinkling lights.

"It's true," thought Torchy,
"there are many kinds of light
in this world. Why should I
hide mine?"
So Torchy flashed his brilliant light.
He flashed and flashed and flashed.
He flashed at building lights,
bridge lights,

street lights and car lights.
He flashed at the moon and the stars.
He flashed all night long.
At last Torchy was tired . . .
tired but so happy . . .

that on his way home
without even thinking,
he began to twinkle.